# THE LEGEND OF
# LIGHTNING LARRY

# THE LEGEND OF
# LIGHTNING LARRY

## AARON SHEPARD
### Pictures by Toni Goffe

CHARLES SCRIBNER'S SONS • NEW YORK
Maxwell Macmillan Canada • Toronto
Maxwell Macmillan International
New York • Oxford • Singapore • Sydney

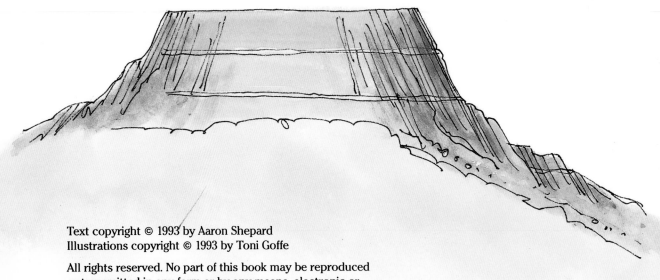

Charles Scribner's Sons Books for Young Readers
Macmillan Publishing Company
866 Third Avenue, New York, NY 10022

Maxwell Macmillan Canada, Inc.
1200 Eglinton Avenue East, Suite 200
Don Mills, Ontario M3C 3N1

Macmillan Publishing Company is part of
the Maxwell Communication Group of Companies.

First edition    10  9  8  7  6  5  4  3  2  1
Printed in Singapore

Library of Congress Cataloging-in-Publication Data
Shepard, Aaron.
    The legend of Lightning Larry /
    Aaron Shepard ; pictures by Toni Goffe. — 1st ed.        p.        cm.
    Summary: Shooting bolts of light instead of bullets, Lightning Larry
changes the town of Brimstone into a friendly, happy place.
    ISBN 0-684-19433-3
1. West (U.S.)—Fiction.    [1. Tall tales.]
I. Goffe, Toni, ill.    II. Title.
PZ7.S5419Le  1993  [E]—dc20        91-43779

For Danny, Cate, and Ishi
—A.S.

To Max, Jeanette, and Tobin
—T.G.

Well, you've heard about gunfighting good guys like Wild Bill Hickok and Wyatt Earp. But I'll tell you a name that strikes even greater fear into the hearts of bad men everywhere.

Lightning Larry.

I'll never forget the day Larry rode into our little town of Brimstone and walked into the Cottonmouth Saloon. He strode up to the bar and smiled straight at the bartender.

"Lemonade, please," he said.

Every head in the place turned to look.

Now, standing next to Larry at the bar was Crooked Curt. Curt was one of a band of rustlers and thieves that had been terrorizing our town, led by a ferocious outlaw named Evil-Eye McNeevil.

Curt was wearing the usual outlaw scowl. Larry turned to him and smiled. "Mighty big frown you got there, mister," he said.

"What's it to you?" growled Curt.

"Well," said Larry, "maybe I could help remove it."

"I'd like to see you try!" said Curt.

The rest of us got out of the way, real fast. The bartender ducked behind the bar. Larry and Curt moved about ten paces from each other, hands at the ready. Larry was still smiling.

Curt moved first. But he only just cleared his gun from its holster before Larry aimed and fired.

*Zing!*

There was no bang and no bullet. Just a little bolt of light that hit Curt right in the heart.

Curt just stood there, his eyes wide with surprise. Then he dropped his gun, and a huge grin spread over his face. He rushed up to Larry and pumped his hand.

"I'm mighty glad to know you, stranger!" he shouted. "The drinks are on me! Lemonade for everyone!"

When Evil-Eye McNeevil and his outlaw gang heard that Crooked Curt had gone straight, they shuddered right down to their boots. Most any outlaw would rather die than smile!

Evil-Eye's men were shook up, but they weren't about to let on. The very next day, Dismal Dan, Devilish Dick, and Dreadful Dave rode into Brimstone, yelling like crazy men and shooting wild. Windows shattered and citizens scattered.

Then Lightning Larry showed up. He never warned them. Never even stopped smiling. Just shot three little bolts of light. Hit those outlaws right in the heart.

Larry's shots knocked the outlaws to the ground. They lay there trying to figure out what had hit them. Then they got up and looked around.

"Looks like we did some damage, boys," said Dismal Dan.

"Hope nobody got hurt," said Devilish Dick.

"We'd better get to work and fix this place up," said Dreadful Dave.

They spent the rest of the day replacing windows and
apologizing to everyone who'd listen. Then, for good measure,
they picked up all the trash in the street.

Evil-Eye McNeevil had lost three more of his meanest men, and he was furious. He decided to do something really nasty.

The next day, Stinky Steve and Sickening Sid walked into the 79th National Savings and Loan with guns in hand. They wore masks, but everyone knew who they were, from the smell.

"Stick up your hands," said Stinky Steve.

"Give us all the money in your vault," ordered Sickening Sid.

They were just backing out the door with the money bags when Lightning Larry strolled by. Didn't even slow his step. Just shot those bandits in the back. Went right through to the heart.

The puzzled outlaws looked at each other.

"Seems a shame to steal the money of hardworking cowboys,"
said Stinky Steve.

"Wouldn't want to make their lives any harder," said Sickening Sid.

They holstered their guns, walked back to the teller, and plunked down the money bags.

"Now, you keep that money safe," said Sickening Sid.

Then they pulled out their wallets and opened up accounts.

That was the last straw for Evil-Eye McNeevil. It was time for a showdown.

The next day, at high noon, Larry was sipping lemonade at the Cottonmouth Saloon. Evil-Eye burst through the doors and stamped up to him.

"I'm Evil-Eye McNeevil," he snarled.

"Hello, Evil-Eye!" said Larry, with a huge smile. "Can I buy you a lemonade?"

"This town ain't big enough for the both of us," said Evil-Eye.

"Seems pretty spacious to me!" said Larry.

"I'll be waiting for you down by the Okey-Dokey Corral," said Evil-Eye, and he stamped out.

Larry finished his lemonade and walked out onto Main Street. Evil-Eye was waiting for him. But Evil-Eye wasn't alone. There on either side of him were Raunchy Ralph and Grimy Greg and Creepy Cal and Moldy Mike and Lousy Luke and Gruesome Gus. And not a one of them looked friendly.

"Nice day for a stroll!" called Larry.

"Draw," said Evil-Eye.

All of us citizens of Brimstone were lining Main Street to see what would happen. Larry was still smiling, but we knew even Larry couldn't outshoot all those outlaws together.

Just then, a voice came from the Cottonmouth Saloon. "Like some help, Larry?"

"Wouldn't mind it!" Larry called back.

Out stepped Crooked Curt. And right behind him were Dismal Dan, Devilish Dick, Dreadful Dave, Stinky Steve, and Sickening Sid. They all took places beside Larry.

"Hello, Evil-Eye!" called Curt.

"Traitors!" yelled Evil-Eye.

"Draw," said Larry, with a smile.

Evil-Eye and his men drew their guns. But Larry and his friends were an eye-blink quicker. Their guns fired seven little bolts of light. Hit those outlaws right in the you-know-what.

"Yippee!" yelled Evil-Eye. He shot in the air.

*Zing!*

There was no bang and no bullet. Just a little bolt of light.

"All right, men!" shouted Larry. "Let's clean up this town, once and for all!"

And before we could duck for cover, Larry and Evil-Eye and the others turned their guns on the rest of us. Bolts of light flew everywhere. No one was spared—not a man, woman, or child.

You never saw such a happy crowd! We all rushed around and pumped each other's hands and hugged each other. Then the musicians got out instruments, and we had dancing, too. Main Street was one huge party, all the rest of that day and on through the night.

I never saw so much lemonade drunk in all my days.

With all the commotion, only a few of us saw Larry ride into the sunset. Can't say where he went. Can't say what he's doing now. But I'll bet he still aims for the heart.